SINGALONG CHART HITS

GW01112031

Published by

WISE PUBLICATIONS
14-15 Berners Street, London W1T 3LJ, UK

Exclusive Distributors:

MUSIC SALES LIMITED
Distribution Centre, Newmarket Road,
Bury St Edmunds, Suffolk IP33 3YB, UK

MUSIC SALES PTY LIMITED
20 Resolution Drive,
Caringbah, NSW 2229, Australia

Order No. AM1002694
ISBN 978-1-84938-958-7

Edited by Lizzie Moore.
Design by Lizzie Barrand.

Printed in the EU

www.musicsales.com

WISE PUBLICATIONS
PART OF THE MUSIC SALES GROUP
LONDON / NEW YORK / PARIS / SYDNEY / COPENHAGEN / BERLIN / MADRID / HONG KONG / TOKYO

TRACK 1

ALL NIGHT LONG

I see everybody around
But it feels like we're in private, ooh
I know you want me so bad
'Cause you just can't seem to hide it, ooh
The lights are movin'
To the rhythm of the music
When we're together
Everything just comes together, baby
So inspired by the moment we can lose it
I hope you're ready

As long as I see the strobe lights
I'm dancing all night long
When we're together, baby
I'm feeling all right
You got me all night long
So tell the D. J. play it
All night long, all night long
So tell the D. J. play it
All night long, all night long
So tell the D. J. play it

Tonight the admission is free
Now we're shuttin' the club down, ooh
We're moving now to the streets
All we got left is love now, ooh
Feel my troubles fading
To the rhythm of your heartbeat
When we're together
Everything just comes together, baby
Every motion calls your name
Baby, once you start me
And I hope you're ready

As long as I see the strobe lights
I'm dancing all night long
When we're together, baby
I'm feeling all right
You got me all night long
So tell the D. J. play it
All night long, all night long
So tell the D. J. play it
All night long, all night long
So tell the D. J. play it

And you make me forget all my worries
Help me put the past behind, ooh
All around us this world's in a hurry
While we stand still in time, ooh
The lights are movin'
To the rhythm of the music
When we're together
Everything just comes together, baby
So inspired by the moment we can lose it
And I hope you're ready

As long as I see the strobe lights
I'm dancing all night long
When we're together, baby
I'm feeling all right
You got me all night long
So tell the D. J. play it
All night long, all night long
So tell the D. J. play it
All night long, all night long
So tell the D. J. play it

It's only you and me together
And this feeling's so strong
Wish I could stay like this forever
All night long, all night long
Said all night long, yeah

TRACK 2

BAD ROMANCE

Oh, caught in a bad romance
Oh, caught in a bad romance
Rah, rah, ah, ah, ah! Roma, Ro-ma-ma
Gaga, ooh-la-la! Want your bad romance
Rah, rah, ah, ah, ah! Roma, Ro-ma-ma
Gaga, ooh-la-la! Want your bad romance

I want your ugly, I want your disease
I want your everything as long as it's free
I want your love
Love, love, love, I want your love
I want your drama, the touch of your hand
I want your leather studded kiss in the sand
I want your love
Love, love, love, I want your love
(Love, love, love, I want your love)

(Spoken:) You know that I want you
And you know that I need you
I want it bad, your bad romance

I want your love and I want your revenge
You and me could write a bad romance, oh
I want your love and all your lovers' revenge
You and me could write a bad romance
Oh, caught in a bad romance
Oh, caught in a bad romance
Rah, rah, ah, ah, ah! Roma, Ro-ma-ma
Gaga, ooh-la-la! Want your bad romance

I want your horror, I want your design
'Cause you're a criminal as long as your mine
I want your love
Love, love, love, I want your love
I want your psycho, your vertigo shtick
While you're in my rear window, baby you're sick
I want your love
Love, love, love, I want your love
(Love, love, love, I want your love)

(Spoken:) You know that I want you
And you know that I need you
I want it bad, your bad romance

Chorus
Rah, rah, ah, ah, ah! Roma, Ro-ma-ma
Gaga, ooh-la-la! Want your bad romance

Walk, walk fashion baby
Work it, move that bit crazy
Walk, walk fashion baby
Work it, move that bit crazy
Walk, walk fashion baby
Work it, move that bit crazy
Walk, walk passion baby
Work it, I'm a freak bit, baby

I want your love and I want your revenge
I want your love, I don't wanna be friends
Je ton amour et je veux ton revenge
Je ton amour, I don't wanna be friends
I don't wanna be friends, I don't wanna be friends
Want your bad romance, caught in a bad romance
Want your bad romance

I want your love and I want your revenge
You and me could write a bad romance, oh
I want your love and all your lovers' revenge
You and me could write a bad romance
Oh, caught in a bad romance
Oh, caught in a bad romance
Rah, rah, ah, ah, ah! Roma, Ro-ma-ma
Gaga, ooh-la-la! Want your bad romance

TRACK 3

BLEEDING LOVE

Closed off from love
I didn't need the pain
Once or twice was enough
And it was all in vain
Time starts to pass
Before you know it you're frozen, ooh

But something happened
For the very first time with you
My heart melted to the ground
Found something true
And everyone's looking 'round
Thinking I'm going crazy
Ooh, yeah, yeah, yeah

But I don't care what they say
I'm in love with you
They try to pull me away
But they don't know the truth
My heart's crippled by the vein
That I keep on closing
You cut me open and I

Keep bleeding, keep, keep bleeding love
I keep bleeding, I keep, keep bleeding love
Keep bleeding, keep, keep bleeding love
You cut me open, ooh

Trying hard not to hear
But they talk so loud
Their piercing sounds fill my ears
Try to fill me with doubt
Yet I know that the goal
Is to keep me from falling

But nothing's greater than the rush
That comes with your embrace
And in this world of loneliness
I see your face
Yet everyone around me
Thinks that I'm going crazy, maybe, maybe

But I don't care what they say
I'm in love with you
They try to pull me away
But they don't know the truth
My heart's crippled by the vein
That I keep on closing
You cut me open and I

Chorus

And it's draining all of me
Oh, they find it hard to believe
I'll be wearing these scars
For everyone to see

I don't care what they say
I'm in love with you
They try to pull me away
But they don't know the truth
My heart's crippled by the vein
That I keep on closing
Ooh, you cut me open and I

Chorus

Keep bleeding, keep, keep bleeding love
I keep bleeding, I keep, keep bleeding love
Keep bleeding, keep, keep bleeding love
You cut me open and I
Keep bleeding, keep, keep bleeding love

TRACK 4

CHASING PAVEMENTS

I've made up my mind
Don't need to think it over
If I'm wrong I am right
Don't need to look no further
This ain't lust
I know this is love, but

If I tell the world
I'll never say enough
'Cause it was not said to you
And that's exactly what I need to do if I
End up with you

Should I give up
Or should I just keep chasing pavements
Even if it leads nowhere?
Or would it be a waste
Even if I knew my place?
Should I leave it there?
Should I give up
Or should I just keep chasing pavements
Even if it leads nowhere?

I build myself up
And fly around in circles
Waiting as my heart drops
And my back begins to tingle
Finally, could this be it or

Should I give up
Or should I just keep chasing pavements
Even if it leads nowhere?
Or would it be a waste
Even if I knew my place?
Should I leave it there?
Should I give up
Or should I just keep chasing pavements
Even if it leads nowhere?

Should I give up
Or should I just keep chasing pavements
Even if it leads nowhere?
Or would it be a waste
Even if I knew my place?
Should I leave it there?
Should I give up?

Or should I just keep on
Chasing pavements?
Should I just keep on
Chasing pavements? Or

Should I give up
Or should I just keep chasing pavements
Even if it leads nowhere?
Or would it be a waste
Even if I knew my place?
Should I leave it there?
Should I give up
Or should I just keep chasing pavements
Even if it leads nowhere?

TRACK 5

EMPIRE STATE OF MIND (PART II) BROKEN DOWN

Ooh, New York
Ooh, New York

Grew up in the town
That is famous as a place of movie scenes
Noise is always loud
There are sirens all around
And the streets are mean

If I can make it here
I can make it anywhere
That's what they say
Seeing my face in lights
Or my name on marquees found
Down on Broadway

Even if it ain't all it seems
I got a pocketful of dreams

Baby, I'm from New York
Concrete jungle where dreams are made of
There's nothing you can't do
Now you're in New York
These streets will make you feel brand new
Big lights will inspire you
Hear it for New York
New York, New York

On the avenue
There ain't never a curfew
Ladies work so hard
Such a melting pot
On the corner selling rock
Preachers pray to God

Hail a gypsy cab
Takes me down from Harlem
To the Brooklyn Bridge
Someone sleeps at night
With a hunger for
More than an empty fridge

I'ma make it by any means
I got a pocketful of dreams

Baby, I'm from New York
Concrete jungle where dreams are made of
There's nothing you can't do
Now you're in New York
These streets will make you feel brand new
Big lights will inspire you
Hear it for New York
New York, New York

One hand in the air for The Big City
Streetlights, big dreams all looking pretty
No place in the world that could compare
Put your lighters in the air
Everybody say, yeah, yeah
Yeah, yeah

New York
Concrete jungle where dreams are made of
There's nothing you can't do
Now you're in New York
These streets will make you feel brand new
Big lights will inspire you
Hear it for New York

TRACK 6

THE FEAR

I wanna be rich
And I want lots of money
I don't care about clever
I don't care about funny
I want loads of clothes
And f*** loads of diamonds
I heard people die
While they're trying to find them

And I'll take my clothes off
And it will be shameless
'Cause everyone knows
It's how you get famous
I'll look at the Sun
And I'll look in the Mirror
I'm on the right track
Yeah, I'm onto a winner

And I don't know what's right
And what's real anymore
And I don't know how I'm meant
To feel anymore
When do you think
It will all become clear?
'Cause I'm being
Taken over by the fear

Life's about film stars
And less about mothers
It's all about fast cars
And cussin' each other
But it doesn't matter
'Cause I'm packing plastic
And that's what makes my life
So f***ing fantastic

And I am a weapon
Of massive consumption
And it's not my fault
It's how I'm programmed to function
I'll look at the Sun
And I'll look in the Mirror
I'm on the right track
Yeah, we're onto a winner

And I don't know what's right
And what's real anymore
And I don't know how I'm meant
To feel anymore
When do you think
It will all become clear?
'Cause I'm being
Taken over by the fear

Forget about guns
And forget ammunition
'Cause I'm killing them all
On my own little mission
Now, I'm not a saint
But I'm not a sinner
And everything's cool
As long as I'm getting thinner

And I don't know what's right
And what's real anymore
And I don't know how I'm meant
To feel anymore
When do you think
It will all become clear?
'Cause I'm being
Taken over by the fear

TRACK 7

FIGHT FOR THIS LOVE

Too much of anything can make you sick
Even the good can be a curse
Makes it hard to know which road to go down
Knowing too much can get you hurt

Is it better, is it worse?
Are we sitting in reverse?
It's just like we're going backwards
I know where I want this to go
Drivin' fast, but let's go slow
What I don't wanna do is crash, no

Just know that you're not in this thing alone
There's always a place in me that you can call home
Whenever you feel like we're growing apart
Let's just go back, back, back, back, back to the start

Anything that's worth having
Is sure enough worth fighting for
Quitting's out of the question
When it gets tough, gotta fight some more
We gotta fight, fight, fight, fight, fight for this love
We gotta fight, fight, fight, fight, fight for this love
We gotta fight, fight, fight, fight, fight for this love
If it's worth having it's worth fighting for, oh

Now every day ain't gon' be no picnic
Love ain't no walk in the park
All you can do is make the best of it now
Can't be afraid of the dark

Just know that you're not in this thing alone
There's always a place in me that you can call home
Whenever you feel like we're growing apart
Let's just go back, back, back, back, back to the start

Anything that's worth having
Is sure enough worth fighting for
Quitting's out of the question
When it gets tough, gotta fight some more
We gotta fight, fight, fight, fight, fight for this love
We gotta fight, fight, fight, fight, fight for this love
We gotta fight, fight, fight, fight, fight for this love
If it's worth having it's worth fighting for, oh

I don't know where we're heading
I'm willing and ready to go
We've been driving so fast
We just need to slow down and just roll

Anything that's worth having
Is sure enough worth fighting for
Quitting's out of the question
When it gets tough, gotta fight some more
We gotta fight, fight, fight, fight, fight for this love
We gotta fight, fight, fight, fight, fight for this love
We gotta fight, fight, fight, fight, fight for this love
If it's worth having it's worth fighting for, oh

We gotta fight, fight, fight, fight, fight for this love
We gotta fight, fight, fight, fight, fight for this love
We gotta fight, fight, fight, fight, fight for this love
If it's worth having it's worth fighting for

TRACK 8

HALO

Remember those walls I built
Well, baby they're tumbling down
And they didn't even put up a fight
They didn't even make a sound
I found a way to let you in
But I never really had a doubt
Standing in the light of your halo
I got my angel now
It's like I've been awakened
Every rule I had you breaking
It's the risk that I'm taking
I ain't never gonna shut you out

Everywhere I'm looking now
I'm surrounded by your embrace
Baby, I can see your halo
You know you're my saving grace
You're everything I need and more
It's written all over your face
Baby, I can feel your halo
Pray it won't fade away

I can feel your halo, halo, halo
I can see your halo, halo, halo
I can feel your halo, halo, halo
I can see your halo, halo, halo

Hit me like a ray of sun
Burning through my darkest night
You're the only one that I want
Think I'm addicted to your light
I swore I'd never fall again
But this don't even feel like falling
Gravity can't forget
To pull me back to the ground again
It's like I've been awakened
Every rule I had you breaking
It's the risk that I'm taking
I'm never gonna shut you out

Everywhere I'm looking now
I'm surrounded by your embrace
Baby, I can see your halo
You know you're my saving grace
You're everything I need and more
It's written all over your face
Baby, I can feel your halo
Pray it won't fade away

I can feel your halo, halo, halo
I can see your halo, halo, halo
I can feel your halo, halo, halo
I can see your halo, halo, halo
(Repeat)

Halo, halo, ooh

Everywhere I'm looking now
I'm surrounded by your embrace
Baby, I can see your halo
You know you're my saving grace
You're everything I need and more
It's written all over your face
Baby, I can feel your halo
Pray it won't fade away

I can feel your halo, halo, halo
I can see your halo, halo, halo
I can feel your halo, halo, halo
I can see your halo, halo, halo
(Repeat)

TRACK 1

HURT

Seems like it was yesterday
When I saw your face
You told me how proud you were
But I walked away
If only I knew
What I know today, ooh, ooh

I would hold you in my arms
I would take the pain away
Thank you for all you've done
Forgive all your mistakes
There's nothing I wouldn't do
To hear your voice again
Sometimes I wanna call you
But I know you won't be there

Whoa, I'm sorry for
Blaming you
For everything
I just couldn't do
And I've hurt myself
By hurting you

Some days I feel broke inside
But I won't admit it
Sometimes I just wanna hide
'Cause it's you I miss
And it's so hard to say goodbye
When it comes to this, ooh

Would you tell me I was wrong?
Would you help me understand?
Are you looking down upon me?
Are you proud of who I am?
There's nothing I wouldn't do
To have just one more chance
To look into your eyes
And see you looking back

Whoa, I'm sorry for
Blaming you
For everything
I just couldn't do
And I've hurt myself, oh

If I had just one more day
I would tell you how much that I've missed you
Since you've been away
Oh, it's dangerous
It's so out of line
To try and turn back time

I'm sorry for
Blaming you
For everything
I just couldn't do
And I've hurt myself
By hurting you

TRACK 2

I KISSED A GIRL

This was never the way I planned
Not my intention
I got so brave, drink in hand
Lost my discretion
It's not what I'm used to
Just wanna try you on
I'm curious for you
Caught my attention

I kissed a girl and I liked it
The taste of her cherry chapstick
I kissed a girl just to try it
I hope my boyfriend don't mind it
It felt so wrong
It felt so right
Don't mean I'm in love tonight
I kissed a girl and I liked it
I liked it

No, I don't even know your name
It doesn't matter
You're my experimental game
Just human nature
It's not what good girls do
Not how they should behave
My head gets so confused
Hard to obey

I kissed a girl and I liked it
The taste of her cherry chapstick
I kissed a girl just to try it
I hope my boyfriend don't mind it
It felt so wrong
It felt so right
Don't mean I'm in love tonight
I kissed a girl and I liked it
I liked it

Us girls, we are so magical
Soft skin, red lips so kissable
Hard to resist, so touchable
Too good to deny it
Ain't no big deal, it's innocent

I kissed a girl and I liked it
The taste of her cherry chapstick
I kissed a girl just to try it
I hope my boyfriend don't mind it
It felt so wrong
It felt so right
Don't mean I'm in love tonight
I kissed a girl and I liked it
I liked it

TRACK 3

LOVE STORY

We were both young when I first saw you
I close my eyes and the flashback starts
I'm standin' there
On a balcony in summer air
See the lights, see the party, the ball gowns
See you make your way
Through the crowd and say hello
Little did I know
That you were Romeo
You were throwing pebbles
And my daddy said stay away from Juliet
And I was cryin' on the staircase
Beggin' you, please don't go

And I said
Romeo, take me somewhere we can be alone
I'll be waiting, all there's left to do is run
You'll be the prince and I'll be the princess
It's a love story, baby, just say yes

So, I sneak out to the garden to see you
We keep quiet 'cause we're dead if they knew
So, close your eyes
Escape this town for a little while
'Cause you were Romeo, I was the scarlet letter
And my daddy said, stay away from Juliet
But you were everything to me
I was beggin' you, please don't go

And I said
Romeo, take me somewhere we can be alone
I'll be waiting, all there's left to do is run
You'll be the prince and I'll be the princess
It's a love story, baby, just say yes

Romeo, save me
They're tryin' to tell me how to feel
This love is difficult, but it's real
Don't be afraid, we'll make it out of this mess
It's a love story, baby, just say yes

I got tired of waiting
Wonderin' if you were ever coming around
My faith in you was fading
When I met you on the outskirts of town

And I said
Romeo, save me, I've been feelin' so alone
I keep waiting for you, but you never come
Is this in my head? I don't know what to think
He knelt to the ground
And pulled out a ring and said

Marry me, Juliet, you never have to be alone
I love you and that's all I really know
I talked to your dad, go pick out a white dress
It's a love story, baby, just say yes
Oh, oh, oh, oh, oh, oh, oh
'Cause we were both young
When I first saw you

TRACK 4

MAMA DO

Uh oh, uh oh
Every night I go
Every night I go sneaking out the door
I lie a little more
Baby I'ma helpless

There's something 'bout the night
And the way it hides
All the things I like
Little black butterflies
Deep inside me

What would my Mama do
Uh oh, uh oh
If she knew 'bout me and you?
Uh oh, uh oh
What would my Daddy say
Uh oh, uh oh
If he saw me hurt this way?
Uh oh, uh oh
Uh oh, uh oh

Why should I feel ashamed?
Feeling guilty at the mention of your name
Here we are again
It's nearly perfect

What would my Mama do
Uh oh, uh oh
If she knew 'bout me and you?
Uh oh, uh oh
What would my Daddy say
Uh oh, uh oh
If he saw me hurt this way?
Uh oh, uh oh

What would my Mama do?
What would my Daddy say?
All the things a girl should know
Are the things she can't control
All the things a girl should know
She can't control

What would my Mama do
Uh oh, uh oh
If she knew 'bout me and you?
Uh oh, uh oh
What would my Daddy say
Uh oh, uh oh
If he saw me hurt this way?
Uh oh, uh oh
Uh oh, uh oh
Uh oh, uh oh
Uh oh, uh oh

TRACK 5

MERCY

Yeah, yeah, yeah
Yeah, yeah, yeah
Yeah, yeah, yeah
Yeah, yeah, yeah

I love you
But I got to stay true
My morals got me on my knees
I beg you, please
Stop playing games
I don't know what this is
But you've got me good
Just like you knew you would
I don't know what you do
But you do it well
I'm under your spell

You got me begging you for mercy
Why won't you release me?
You got me begging you for mercy
Why won't you release me?
I said release me

Now you think that I
Will be something on the side
But you've got to understand
That I need a man who can take my hand
Yes I do
I don't know what this is
But you've got me good
Just like you knew you would
I don't know what you do
But you do it well
I'm under your spell

You got me begging you for mercy
Why won't you release me?
You got me begging you for mercy
Why won't you release me?
I said you better release me

I'm begging you for mercy
Just why won't you release me?
I'm begging you for mercy
You got me begging
You got me begging
You got me begging

Mercy, why won't you release me?
I'm begging you for mercy
Why won't you release me?
You've got me begging you for mercy, yeah
I'm begging you for mercy
I'm begging you for mercy
I'm begging you for mercy
I'm begging you for mercy
Why won't you release me? Yeah

(Spoken:) Break it down

You got me begging
Begging you for mercy
You got me begging
Down on my knees
I said, you got me begging
Begging you for mercy
You got me begging

TRACK 6

POKER FACE

I wanna hold 'em like they do in Texas please
Fold 'em, let 'em hit me, raise it, baby, stay with me
Luck and intuition play the cards with spades to start
And after he's been hooked
I'll play the one that's on his heart

Oh, whoa, oh, oh, oh, oh, oh
I'll get him hot, show him what I got
Oh, whoa, oh, oh, oh, oh, oh
I'll get him hot, show him what I got

Can't read my, can't read my
No, he can't read my poker face
(She's got to love nobody)
Can't read my, can't read my
No, he can't read my poker face
(She's got to love nobody)
P p p poker face, p p poker face
P p p poker face, p p poker face

I wanna roll with him, a hard pair we will be
A little gamblin' is fun when you're with me
Russian Roulette is not the same without a gun
And, baby, when it's love, if it's not rough it isn't fun

Oh, whoa, oh, oh, oh, oh, oh
I'll get him hot, show him what I got
Oh, whoa, oh, oh, oh, oh, oh
I'll get him hot, show him what I got

Can't read my, can't read my
No, he can't read my poker face
(She's got to love nobody)
Can't read my, can't read my
No, he can't read my poker face
(She's got to love nobody)
P p p poker face, p p poker face
P p p poker face, p p poker face

I won't tell you that I love you
Kiss or hug you
'Cause I'm bluffin' with my muffin
I'm not lyin', I'm just stunnin'
With my love glue gunnin'
Just like a chick in the casino
Take your bank before I pay you out
I promise this, promise this
Check this hand, 'cause I'm marvelous

Can't read my, can't read my
No, he can't read my poker face
(She's got to love nobody)
Can't read my, can't read my
No, he can't read my poker face
(She's got to love nobody)
(Sing 3 times)

P p p poker face, p p poker face
P p p poker face, p p poker face
(Sing 3 times)

TRACK 7

SO WHAT

Na na na na na na na na na na na na na
Na na na na na na na na na na na na na
I guess I just lost my husband
I don't know where he went
So I'm gonna drink my money
I'm not gonna pay his rent
I gotta brand new attitude
And I'm gonna wear it tonight
I'm gonna get in trouble
I wanna start a fight
Na na na na na na na
I wanna start a fight
Na na na na na na na
I wanna start a fight

So, so what? I'm still a rock star
I got my rock moves and I don't need you
And guess what? I'm having more fun
And now that we're done
I'm gonna show you tonight
I'm alright, I'm just fine
And you're a tool
So, so what? I am a rock star
I got my rock moves
And I don't want you tonight

(Spoken:) Uh, check my flow, oh

The waiter just took my table
And gave it to Jessica Simps...
I guess I'll go sit with drum boy
At least he'll know how to hit
What if this song's on the radio
Then somebody's gonna die
I'm gonna get in trouble
My ex will start a fight
Na na na na na na na
He's gonna start a fight
Na na na na na na na
We're all gonna get in a fight

Chorus

You weren't there, you never were
You want it all but that's not fair
I gave you life, I gave my all
You weren't there, you let me fall

So, so what? I'm still a rock star
I got my rock moves and I don't need you
And guess what? I'm having more fun
And now that we're done
I'm gonna show you tonight
I'm alright, I'm just fine
And you're a tool
So, so what? I am a rock star
I got my rock moves
And I don't want you tonight

I'm gonna show you tonight
I'm alright, I'm just fine
And you're a tool
So, so what? I am a rock star
I got my rock moves
And I don't want you tonight

Ba da da da da da

TRACK 8

TAKE A BOW

Oh, how 'bout a round of applause?
Yeah, standing ovation?
Ooh, yeah, yeah, yeah, yeah, yeah

You look so dumb right now
Standing outside my house
Trying to apologise
You're so ugly when you cry
Please! Just cut it out

Don't tell me you're sorry 'cause you're not
Baby, when I know you're only sorry you got caught

But you put on quite a show
Really had me going
But now it's time to go
Curtain's finally closing
That was quite a show
Very entertaining
But it's over now
Go on and take a bow, oh

Grab your clothes and get gone
You'd better hurry up
Before the sprinklers come on
Talking 'bout, "Girl I love you, you're the one"
This just looks like a rerun
Please! What else is on?

And don't tell me you're sorry 'cause you're not
Baby, when I know you're only sorry you got caught

But you put on quite a show
Really had me going
But now it's time to go
Curtain's finally closing
That was quite a show
Very entertaining
But it's over now
Go on and take a bow, oh

And the award for
The best lie goes to you
For making me believe
That you could be faithful to me
Let's hear your speech, oh

How 'bout a round of applause?
Standing ovation?

But you put on quite a show
Really had me going
Now it's time to go
Curtain's finally closing
That was quite a show
Very entertaining
But it's over now
Go on and take a bow
But it's over now

TRACK LISTING

CD1

1. ALL NIGHT LONG
Words & Music by Rico Love, James Scheffer, Samuel Watters & Louis Biancaniello

**© Copyright 2009 Rico Love Is Still A Rapper/ Foray Music/Jimipub Music/EMI Blackwood Music Incorporated/ Breakthrough Creations/EMI April Music Incorporated/S M Y/ Sony/ATV Tunes LLC, USA.
EMI Music Publishing Limited (75%)/
Sony/ATV Music Publishing (25%).
All Rights Reserved. International Copyright Secured.**

(Love/Scheffer/Watters/Biancaniello)
EMI Music Publishing Limited/Sony/ATV Music Publishing (UK) Limited

2. BAD ROMANCE
Words & Music by Stefani Germanotta & RedOne

**© Copyright 2009 House Of Gaga Publishing Incorporated/ Sony/ATV Songs LLC, USA.
Sony/ATV Music Publishing.
All Rights Reserved. International Copyright Secured.**

(Germanotta/RedOne)
Sony/ATV Music Publishing (UK) Limited

3. BLEEDING LOVE
Words & Music by Ryan Tedder & Jesse McCartney

**© Copyright 2007 Write 2 Live Publishing/Jambition Music, USA.
Kobalt Music Publishing Limited (66.67%)/
Warner/Chappell Artemis Music Limited (33.33%).
All Rights Reserved. International Copyright Secured.**

(Tedder/McCartney)
Kobalt Music Publishing Limited/Warner/Chappell Artemis Music Limited

4. CHASING PAVEMENTS
Words & Music by Adele & Eg White

**© Copyright 2007 Universal Music Publishing Limited.
All rights in Germany administered by Universal Music Publ. GmbH.
All Rights Reserved. International Copyright Secured.**

(Adele/White)
Universal Music Publishing Limited

5. EMPIRE STATE OF MIND (PART II) BROKEN DOWN
Words & Music by Alicia Keys, Sylvia Robinson, Shawn Carter, Angela Hunte, Bert Keyes, Alexander Shuckburgh & Janet Sewell

**© Copyright 2010 EMI Music Publishing Limited (50%)/
IQ Music Limited (40%)/Global Talent Publishing (10%).
All Rights Reserved. International Copyright Secured.**

(Keyes/Robinson/Carter/Hunte/Keyes/Shuckburgh/Sewell)
EMI Music Publishing Limited/IQ Music Limited/Global Talent Publishing

6. THE FEAR
Words & Music by Lily Allen & Greg Kurstin

**© Copyright 2008 Universal Music Publishing Limited (50%)
(administered in Germany by Universal Music Publ. GmbH)/
EMI Music Publishing Limited (50%).
All Rights Reserved. International Copyright Secured.**

(Allen/Kurstin)
Universal Music Publishing Limited/EMI Music Publishing Limited

7. FIGHT FOR THIS LOVE
Words & Music by Steve Kipner, Wayne Wilkins & Andre Merritt

**© Copyright 2009 Blow The Speakers/Sony/ATV Music Publishing (33.34%)/
Sonic Graffiti/EMI Music Publishing Limited (33.34%)/
Universal Music Publishing Limited (16.66%)
(administered in Germany by Universal Music Publ. GmbH)/
Ms Lynn Publishing/Universal/MCA Music Limited (16.66%)
(administered in Germany by Universal/MCA Music Publ. GmbH).
All Rights Reserved. International Copyright Secured.**

(Wilkins/Merritt)
Sony/ATV Music Publishing (UK) Limited/EMI Music Publishing Limited/ Universal Music Publishing Limited/Universal/MCA Music Limited

8. HALO
Words & Music by Ryan Tedder, Beyoncé Knowles & Evan Bogart

**© Copyright 2008 Write 2 Live Publishing/Sony/ATV Songs LLC/
EMI April Music Incorporated/B Day Publishing, USA.
Kobalt Music Publishing Limited (60%)/Sony/ATV Music Publishing (25%)/
EMI Music Publishing Limited (15%).
All Rights Reserved. International Copyright Secured.**

(Tedder/Knowles/Bogart)
Kobalt Music Publishing Limited/ Sony/ATV Music Publishing (UK) Limited/ EMI Music Publishing Limited

CD2

1. HURT
Words & Music by Linda Perry, Christina Aguilera & Mark Ronson

**© Copyright 2006 Stuck In The Throat/Famous Music LLC/Xtina Music/ Careers-BMG Music Publishing Incorporated, USA.
Sony/ATV Harmony (UK) Limited (65%)/
Universal Music Publishing International Limited (14%)/
Universal Music Publishing MGB Limited (14%)/
EMI Music Publishing Limited (7%).
All Rights Reserved. International Copyright Secured.**

(Perry/Aguilera/Ronson)
Sony/ATV Harmony (UK) Limited/Universal Music Publishing International Limited/ Universal Music Publishing MGB Limited/EMI Music Publishing Limited

2. I KISSED A GIRL
Words & Music by Katy Perry, Lukasz Gottwald, Max Martin & Cathy Dennis

**© Copyright 2008 Maratone AB/Kasz Money Publishing/Prescription Songs LLC/
Kobalt Music Publishing Limited (56.25%)/EMI Music Publishing Limited (25%)/
When I'm Rich You'll Be My Bitch/Warner/Chappell Music North America Limited (18.75%).
All Rights Reserved. International Copyright Secured.**

(Perry/Gottwald/Martin/Dennis)
Kobalt Music Publishing Limited/EMI Music Publishing Limited/ Warner/Chappell Music North America Limited

3. LOVE STORY
Words & Music by Taylor Swift

**© Copyright 2008 Taylor Swift Music/Sony/ATV Tree Publishing.
Sony/ATV Music Publishing.
All Rights Reserved. International Copyright Secured.**

(Swift)
Sony/ATV Music Publishing (UK) Limited

4. MAMA DO
Words & Music by Phil Thornalley & Mads Hauge

**© Copyright 2008 Universal Music Publishing MGB Limited.
All rights in Germany administered by Musik Edition Discoton GmbH
(a division of Universal Music Publishing Group).
All Rights Reserved. International Copyright Secured.**

(Thornalley/Hauge)
Universal Music Publishing MGB Limited

5. MERCY
Words & Music by Duffy & Stephen Booker

**© Copyright 2007 EMI Music Publishing Limited (60%)/
Universal Music Publishing Limited (40%)
(administered in Germany by Universal Music Publ. GmbH).
All Rights Reserved. International Copyright Secured.**

(Duffy/Booker)
EMI Music Publishing Limited/Universal Music Publishing Limited

6. POKER FACE
Words & Music by Stefani Germanotta & Nadir Khayat

**© Copyright 2008 Sony/ATV Music Publishing.
All Rights Reserved. International Copyright Secured.**

(Germanotta/Khayat)
Sony/ATV Music Publishing (UK) Limited

7. SO WHAT
Words & Music by Max Martin, Alecia Moore & Johan Schuster

**© Copyright 2008 Pink Inside Publishing/Maratone, AB.
EMI Music Publishing Limited (33.33%)/Kobalt Music Publishing Limited (66.67%).
All Rights Reserved. International Copyright Secured.**

(Martin/Moore/Schuster)
EMI Music Publishing Limited/Kobalt Music Publishing Limited

8. TAKE A BOW
Words & Music by Mikkel Eriksen, Tor Erik Hermansen & Shaffer Smith

**© Copyright 2008 Imagem Music (50%)/EMI Music Publishing Limited (25%)/
Sony/ATV Music Publishing (25%).
All Rights Reserved. International Copyright Secured.**

(Eriksen/Hermansen/Smith)
Imagem Music/EMI Music Publishing Limited/Sony/ATV Music Publishing (UK) Limited

**THE INCLUDED CDS CAN BE PLAYED ON A CD PLAYER OR A COMPUTER.
WHEN YOU OPEN THE CD ON THE COMPUTER, YOU'LL FIND AN ADDITIONAL DATA FILE.**